Seasons Change Like l̶i̶t̶t̶l̶e̶ ̶M̶e̶

A Story f̶

For Mary and John Hamilton,
who knew me when I was a little lion in a big world.
Whose love and support has seen me through many changes.
I hold you both in my heart wherever I go.

My name is Roary and I wrote this rhyme.
I look at the seasons, I write about time.
Changes will happen, and change can be good.
Life will move on and unfold as it should.

I jumped off the toy shelf not too long ago.
There were many things that I wanted to know.
Why does the weather turn cold and then hot?
Why do the leaves fall, like it or not?!

Changes are happening morning and night.
I cannot stop them, try as I might.
Part of the year is sunny and nice.
Then it starts changing to cold days with ice.

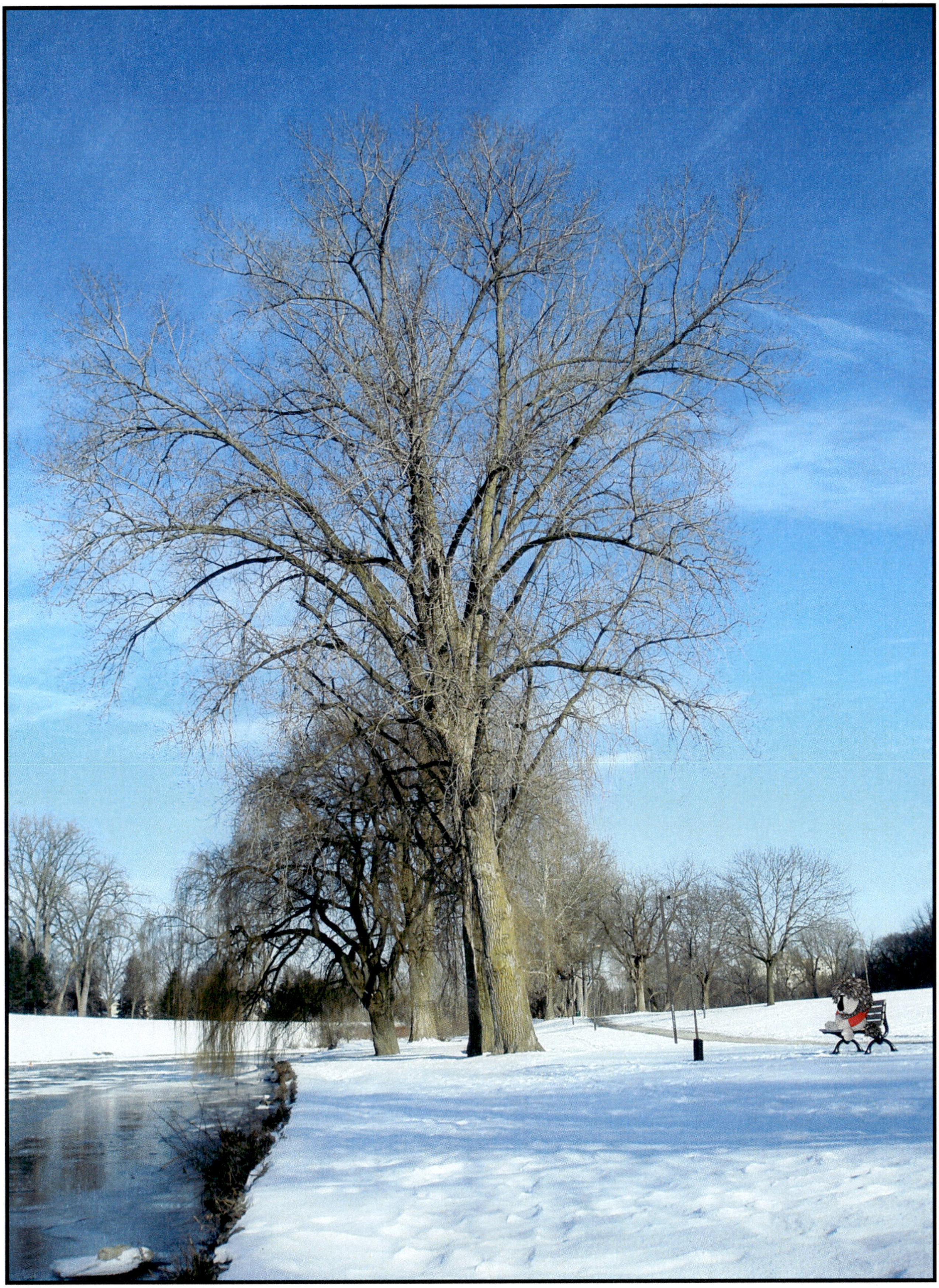

There are four seasons a new year will bring.
There is **summer** and **fall** and **winter** and **spring**.
Each one is grand in its own special way.
The passing of time brings change to each day.

Summer is filled with blue sky and sun,
picnics and parties and holiday fun.
Fishing and swimming and campfire songs,
relaxing outside 'cause the days are so long.

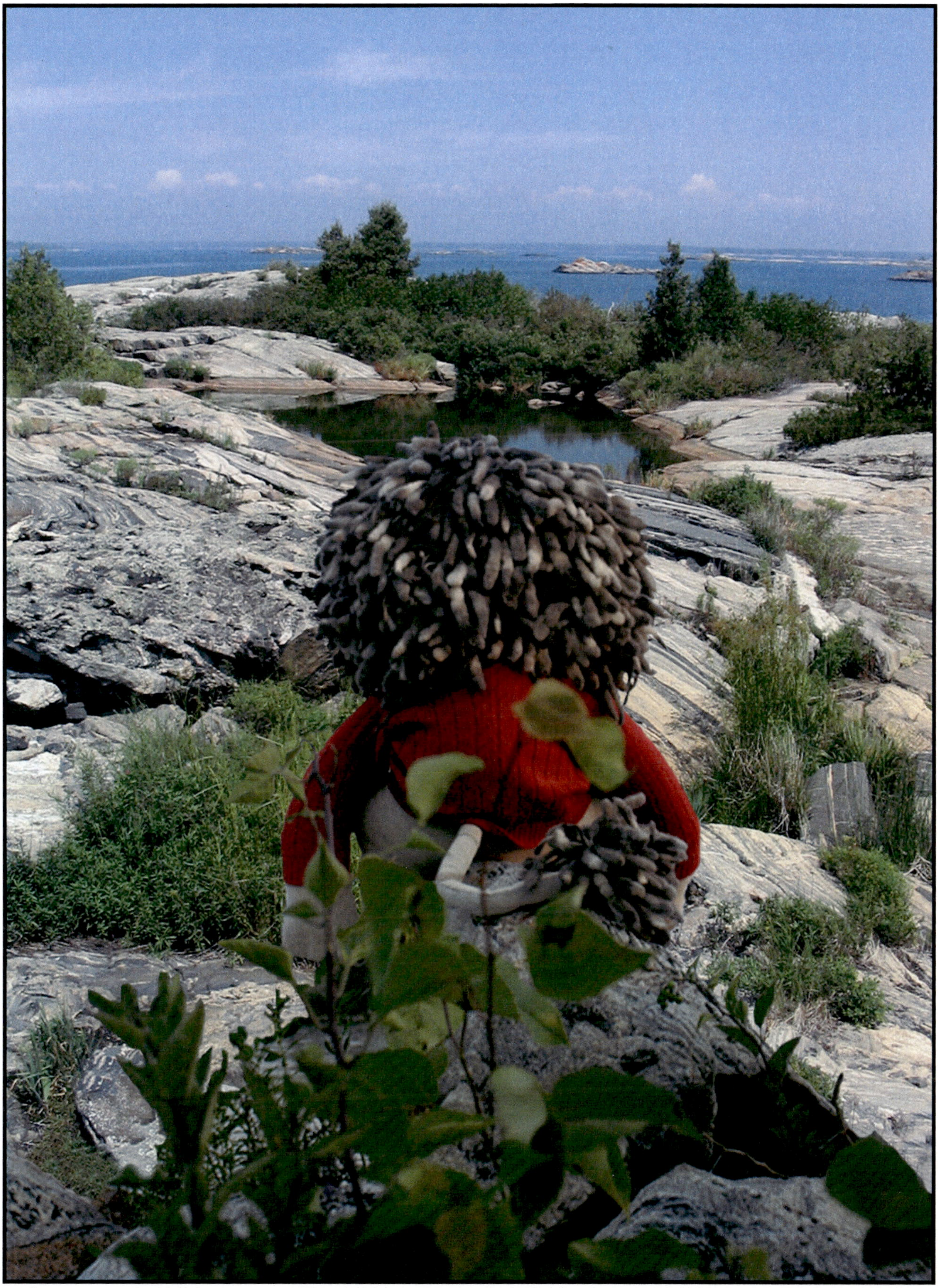

Diving off docks and speedy bike riding,
popsicles, lemonade, water-park-sliding.
Sleeping in tents and gazing at stars,
canoeing, rock-skipping, convertible cars.

Summer is time to take a long break,
to look at the flowers, the trees and the lake.
It's time to let loose and get out in the heat;
bright summer days are a tough thing to beat.

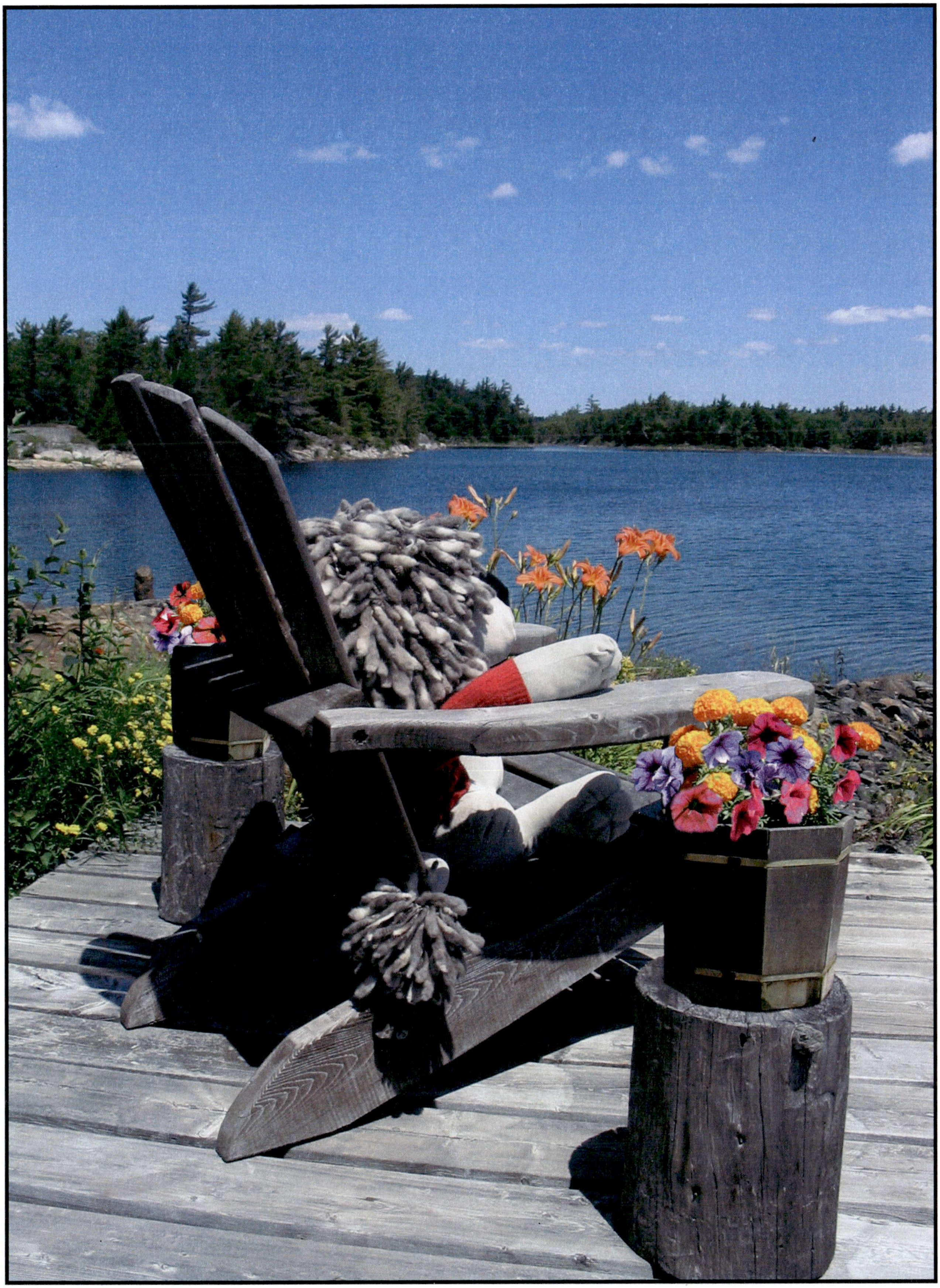

After the summer the weather gets cooler.
Back to school time with a pencil and ruler.
Old friends are found and new friends are made.
Hopscotch and skipping and marbles are played.

Fall is the time when the air can get brisk.
It soon smells like pumpkins and hot apple crisp.
Climbing up trees and jumping in leaves,
singing while wiping your nose on your sleeves.

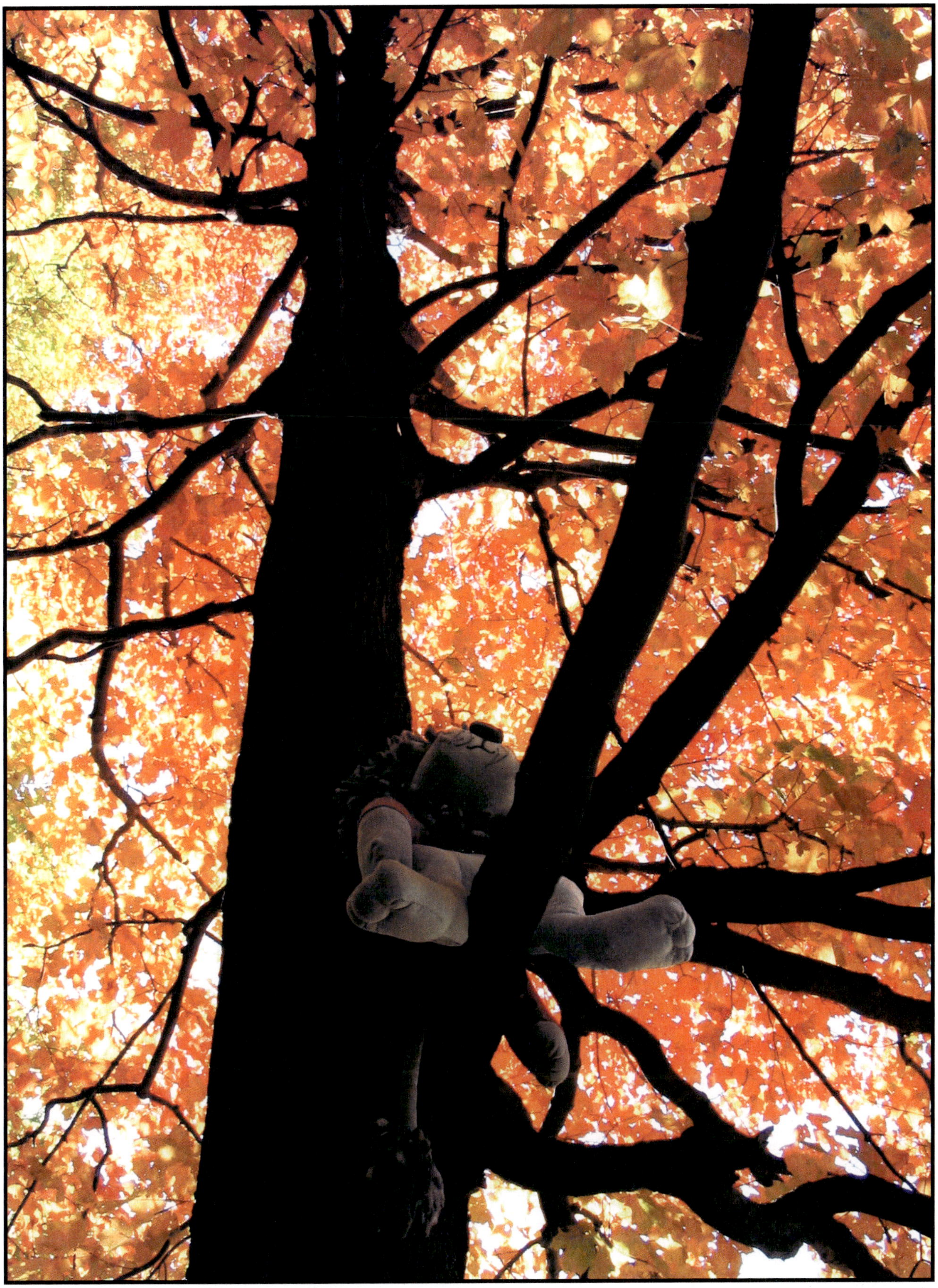

Fall winds blow from the north and the west.
It's nature's own way of preparing to rest.
Beautiful colours bring fall to an end.
It's time to give thanks for family and friends.

Winter is time to play in the snow,
to watch the flakes fall and hear the storms blow.
Skating and sledding and skiing down hills,
hot chocolate waiting to warm up the chills.

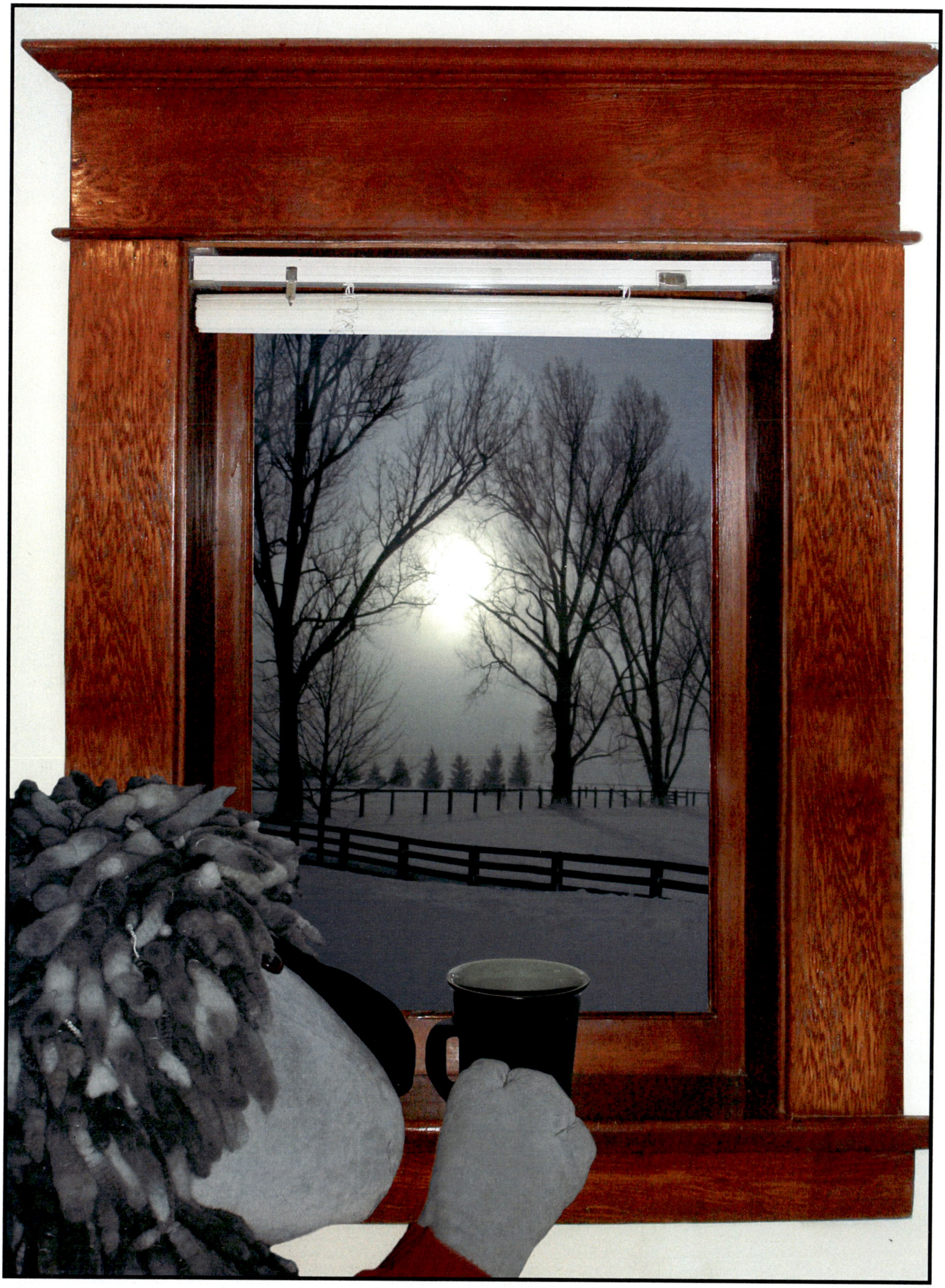

Icicles, candy canes, thick wooly socks,
snowlions, mittens and long winter walks.
For some the cold months are hard to withstand.
For others the winter's a white wonderland.

Once the snow melts and birds build their nests,
nature awakes from her long winter rest.
The rain starts to fall and the thunder is awesome.
The showers allow for the flowers to blossom.

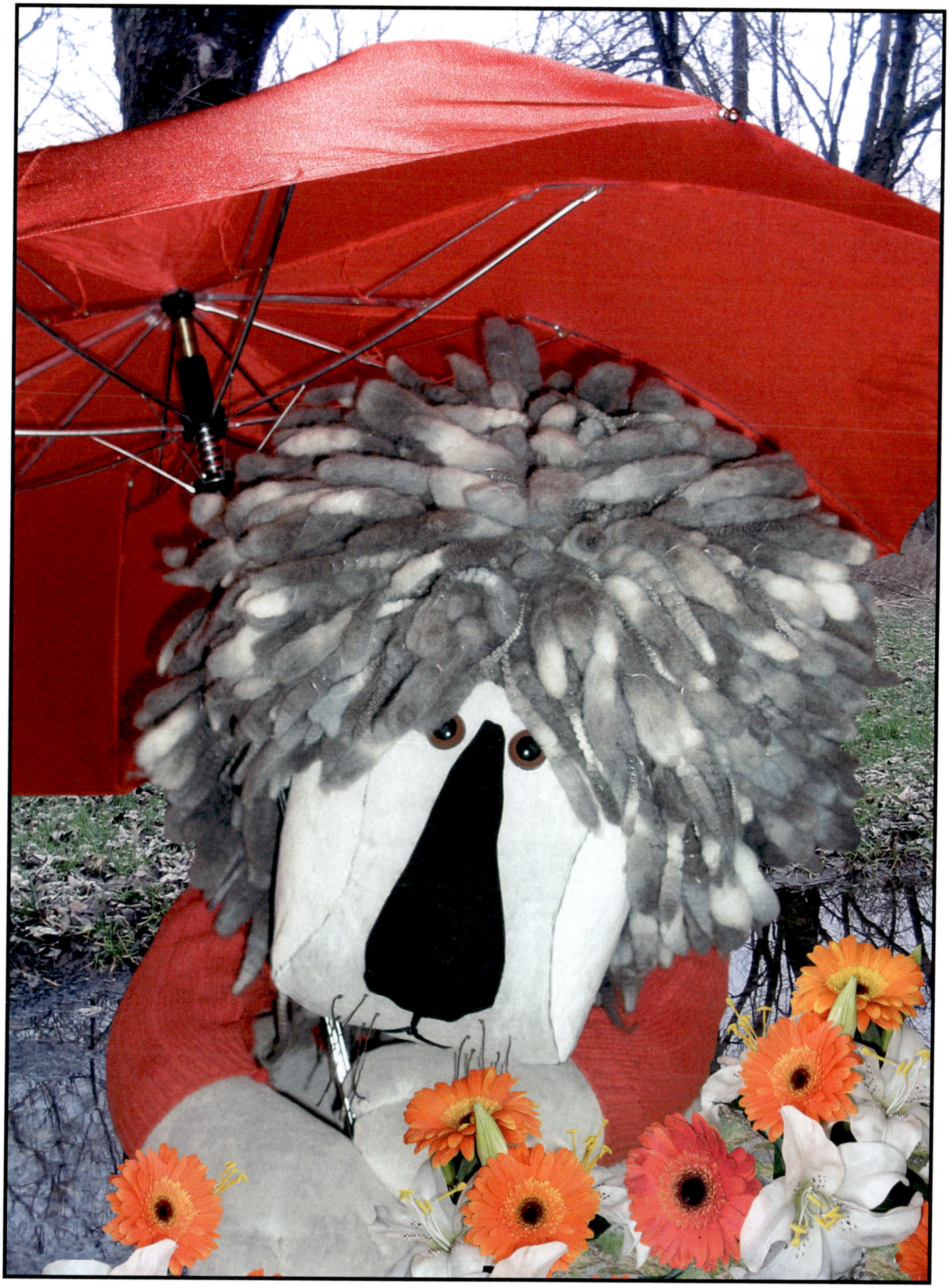

Spring is a time to smell the fresh air.
Take off your toque 'cause the weather is fair.
Jumping in puddles and buds on the trees,
butterflies playing with striped bumble bees.

Now that I know that change can be great,
I'm no longer scared of change that awaits.
A change will end one thing; but this is all right.
A brand new beginning will soon be in sight.

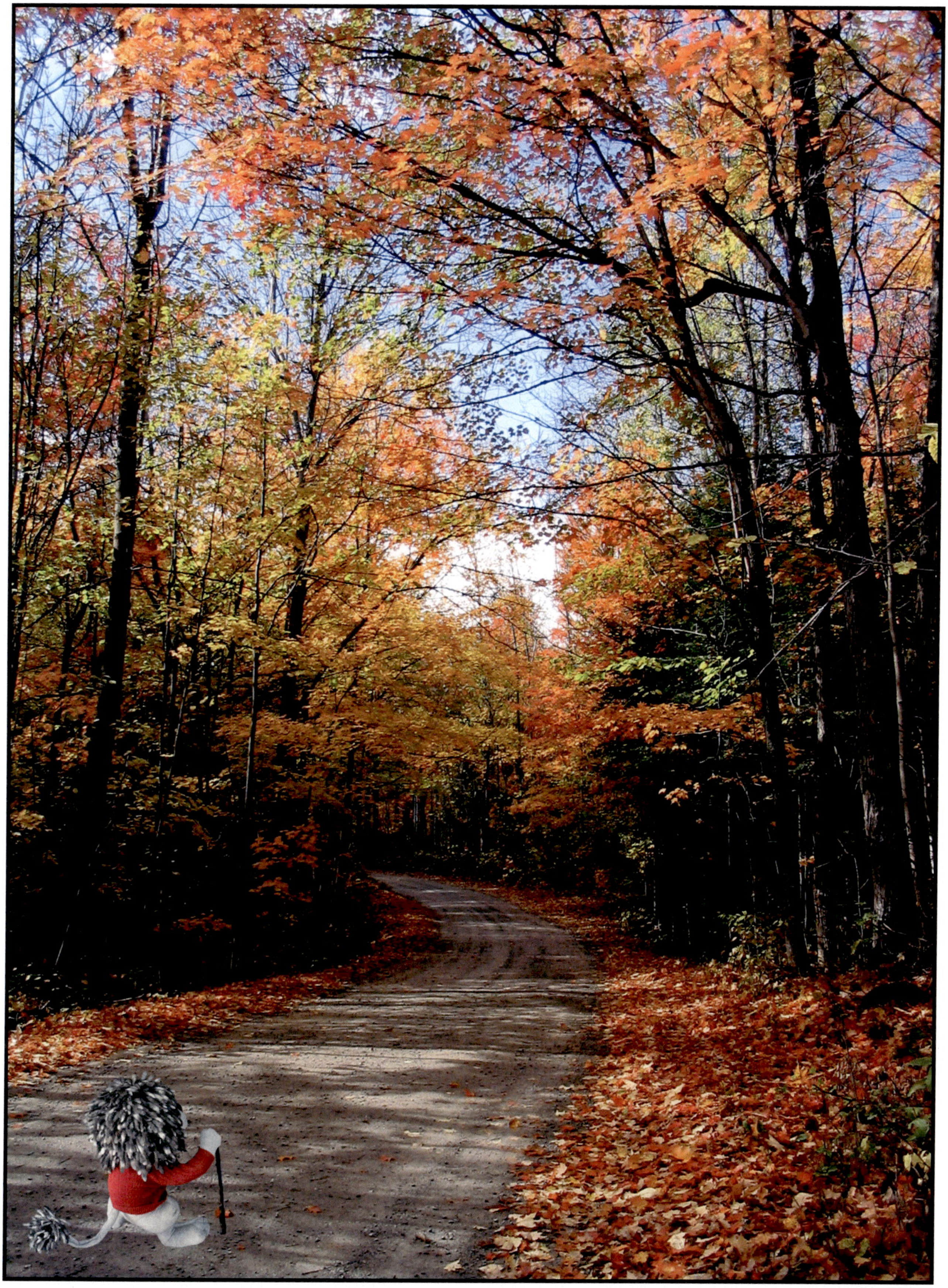

Just like the seasons you will change too,
from hobbies to hairdos to sizes of shoe.
Change can come quickly, and change can come slow.
But one thing is certain; you'll change as you grow.

The place you call home may change with the times.
You'll change what you buy with your dollars and dimes.
A time will come soon when you change how you dress.
And one day your room might be less of a mess.

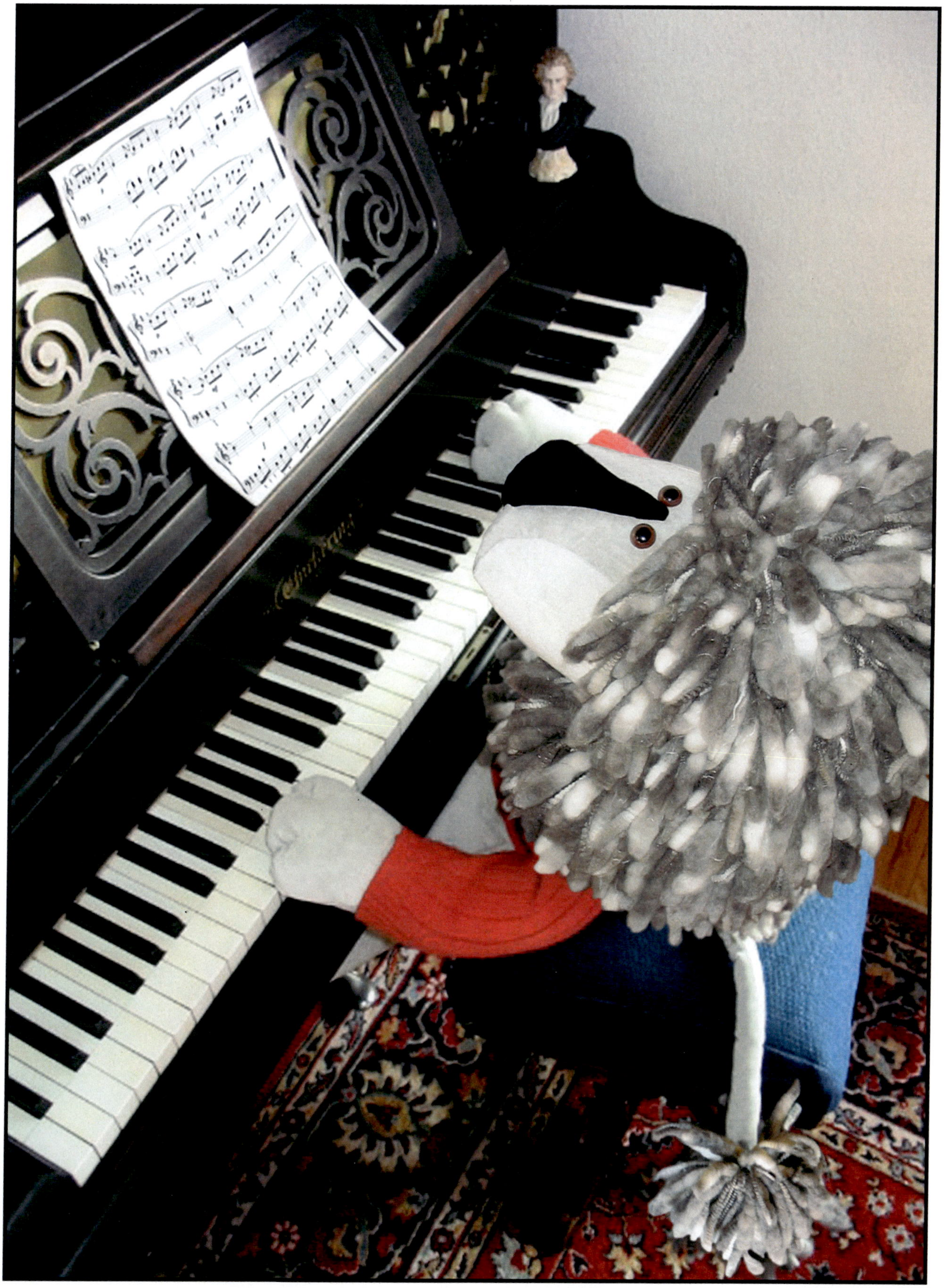

There are some changes that take a long while,
like finishing school and finding your style.
But then there are changes that happen quite fast,
like losing a tooth, or getting a cast.

I may be a lion and stuffed as can be,
but there are still changes I feel and I see.
One thing I've learned and this I can't hide,
when change is *accepted* you feel good inside.

If a change makes you worried or angry or sad,
think of the seasons... change isn't so bad.
Let the change happen, enjoy what is new.
Smile and let change create a new you!

In order to grow, change needs to take place.
It's one fact of life that you'll need to embrace.
Take it from me, a lion who knows...
with every new change, your heart and soul grows.

© Copyright 2007 Roary.

All rights reserved. No part of this publication may be reproduced, stored in a retrieval system, or transmitted, in any form or by any means, electronic, mechanical, photocopying, recording, or otherwise, without the written prior permission of the author.

Note for Librarians: A cataloguing record for this book is available from Library and Archives Canada at www.collectionscanada. ca/amicus/index-e.html
ISBN 1-4251-1992-1

Printed in Victoria, BC, Canada. Printed on paper with minimum 30% recycled fibre.
Trafford's print shop runs on "green energy" from solar, wind and other environmentally-friendly power sources.

Offices in Canada, USA, Ireland and UK

Book sales for North America and international:
Trafford Publishing, 6E–2333 Government St.,
Victoria, BC V8T 4P4 CANADA
phone 250 383 6864 (toll-free 1 888 232 4444)
fax 250 383 6804; email to orders@trafford.com

Book sales in Europe:
Trafford Publishing (UK) Limited, 9 Park End Street, 2nd Floor
Oxford, UK OX1 1HH UNITED KINGDOM
phone +44 (0)1865 722 113 (local rate 0845 230 9601)
facsimile +44 (0)1865 722 868; info.uk@trafford.com

Order online at:
trafford.com/07-0397

10 9 8 7 6 5 4 3